A Note to Parents and Caregivers:

Read-it! Readers are for children who are just starting on the amazing road to reading. These beautiful books support both the acquisition of reading skills and the love of books.

The RED LEVEL presents familiar topics using common words and repeating sentence patterns.
The BLUE LEVEL presents new ideas using a larger vocabulary and varied sentence structure.
The YELLOW LEVEL presents more challenging ideas, a broad vocabulary, and wide variety in sentence structure.

When sharing a book with your child, read in short stretches, pausing often to talk about the pictures. Have your child turn the pages and point to the pictures and familiar words. And be sure to reread favorite stories or parts of stories.

There is no right or wrong way to share books with children. Find time to read with your child, and pass on the legacy of literacy.

Adria F. Klein, Ph.D.
Professor Emeritus
California State University
San Bernardino, California

First American edition published in 2003 by
Picture Window Books
5115 Excelsior Boulevard
Suite 232
Minneapolis, MN 55416
1-877-845-8392
www.picturewindowbooks.com

First published in Great Britain by Franklin Watts, 96 Leonard Street, London, EC2A 4XD
Text © Margaret Nash 2000
Illustration © Jörg Saupe 2000

Printed in the United States of America.

Library of Congress Cataloging-in-Publication Data
Nash, Margaret.
  The best snowman / by Margaret Nash ; illustrated by Jörg Saupe.—1st American ed.
    p. cm. — (Read-it! readers)
  Summary: When Robby builds a different snowman for each of his neighbors, Mr. Perry
thinks that his teeny-weeny snowman is the best.
  ISBN 1-4048-0048-4
  [1. Snowmen—Fiction.] I. Saupe, Jörg, ill. II. Title. III. Series.
  PZ7.N1732 Be 2003
  [E]—dc21   2002072290

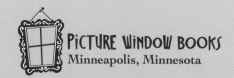

PICTURE WINDOW BOOKS
Minneapolis, Minnesota

The Best Snowman

Written by Margaret Nash

Illustrated by Jörg Saupe

Reading Advisors:
Adria F. Klein, Ph.D.
Professor Emeritus, California State University
San Bernardino, California

Ruth Thomas
Durham Public Schools
Durham, North Carolina

R. Ernice Bookout
Durham Public Schools
Durham, North Carolina

Picture Window Books
Minneapolis, Minnesota

Robby had never seen snow.
Then, one cold day, it came.

Robby made a snowman
as fat as a barrel.

Then he stuck a pot on its head.

"He's funny," said Mr. Jones,
who lived next door.

"Can you make one for me, too?"

9

"And me," said Mrs. Cook.

"And us," said Miss Ling
and Mr. Perry.

"OK," said Robby.

"I'll make snowmen for all of you."

"One like yours, please,"
said Mr. Jones.

"As fat as a barrel!"

The snowman was a very
funny shape.

But Mr. Jones was pleased.

"A tall, thin one, please," said Miss Ling.

The snowman was so tall and thin, it couldn't stand up. But Miss Ling was pleased.

"I'd like a snow-woman, please," said Mrs. Cook.

The hat was much too big
for the snow-woman.
But Mrs. Cook was pleased.

Robby came to the
last house.

23

"A teeny-weeny snowman, please," said Mr. Perry.

"They're the best."

So, Robby made a snowman the size of a snowball.

"Why is he the best?" asked Robby.

Mr. Perry took the
teeny-weeny snowman

and put him in the freezer
with the frozen peas.

"He's the best snowman because he won't melt," said Mr. Perry.

And he didn't!

Red Level

The Best Snowman, by Margaret Nash 1-4048-0048-4
Bill's Baggy Pants, by Susan Gates 1-4048-0050-6
Cleo and Leo, by Anne Cassidy 1-4048-0049-2
Felix on the Move, by Maeve Friel 1-4048-0055-7
Jasper and Jess, by Anne Cassidy 1-4048-0061-1
The Lazy Scarecrow, by Jillian Powell 1-4048-0062-X
Little Joe's Big Race, by Andy Blackford 1-4048-0063-8
The Little Star, by Deborah Nash 1-4048-0065-4
The Naughty Puppy, by Jillian Powell 1-4048-0067-0
Selfish Sophie, by Damian Kelleher 1-4048-0069-7

Blue Level

The Bossy Rooster, by Margaret Nash 1-4048-0051-4
Jack's Party, by Ann Bryant 1-4048-0060-3
Little Red Riding Hood, by Maggie Moore 1-4048-0064-6
Recycled!, by Jillian Powell 1-4048-0068-9
The Sassy Monkey, by Anne Cassidy 1-4048-0058-1
The Three Little Pigs, by Maggie Moore 1-4048-0071-9

Yellow Level

Cinderella, by Barrie Wade 1-4048-0052-2
The Crying Princess, by Anne Cassidy 1-4048-0053-0
Eight Enormous Elephants, by Penny Dolan 1-4048-0054-9
Freddie's Fears, by Hilary Robinson 1-4048-0056-5
Goldilocks and the Three Bears, by Barrie Wade 1-4048-0057-3
Mary and the Fairy, by Penny Dolan 1-4048-0066-2
Jack and the Beanstalk, by Maggie Moore 1-4048-0059-X
The Three Billy Goats Gruff, by Barrie Wade 1-4048-0070-0